The Corgi that Came for Christmas

N. W. Nelson

DEDICATION

This book is dedicated to my spouse, our two daughters and our two Corgis who are my inspiration for this story.

About Pembroke Welsh Corgis

The Pembroke Welsh Corgi is a herding dog breed. They originate from Wales. They live to be 12 to 14 years old. Their average weight is between 25 to 30 lbs. They are spirited little dogs and although they have short legs they are very quick and athletic. They are a loyal and dependable family pet.

They tend to be a bit bossy with young children but are friendly and protective of their family. They love to bark, bark, bark but also love to please their master. If you would like a lifelong companion and have the time to dedicate to a dog this breed might be wonderful addition to your family.

The Corgi that came for Christmas

CONTENTS

ACKNOWLEDGMENTS

Thank you to my editor, Meghan Nelson, for her attention to detail and expertise in English.

CHAPTER 1
WHO IS THIS CORGI?

Boomer lazily opened one eye and yawned, stretching his stubby legs out in front of him. His brown and white legs stretched upward as his white chest touched the ground. He turned one black and brown ear to listen for the sound of his mother coming in from the barn.

Boomer was a Pembroke Welsh Corgi puppy. This really didn't mean anything to him, but if someone were to look at him they would notice that his legs were extremely short and his tail was missing. His sisters started jumping around in the large wooden box that they slept in.

The back door opened and his mother walked into the warm kitchen in front of the lady of the house. The leaves had fallen off the trees a few weeks ago and a cold rain had been falling all week. It was warm in the farmhouse and the Corgi pups were allowed to run around the kitchen when the morning chores were done.

Boomer received a soft lick from his mother. Her fur was reddish brown and white, her eyes were bright, and her ears upright. Boomer had four sisters that looked like his mother. Two of them had already gone to new homes. Each afternoon people had been coming to the house and looking at the puppies. Each day Boomer would hide in the corner as his sisters ran around looking adorable.

Boomer was the only boy in the litter, but he was also the smallest and most shy. He often thought to himself that he was not beautiful like his mom and his sisters. They were a reddish brown and white but instead he was a tricolor Corgi like his father.

Boomer's father was a working corgi and he was mostly black with white and brown fur mixed in. He helped herd the black Angus cattle on the farm. His father lived in a nice kennel in the barn and never came into the house.

Today a family came and looked at his remaining two sisters. The two beautiful sisters jumped around and looked adorable as usual wagging their little nubby tails and giving everyone lots of kisses. The family had two boys, so they decided to take both girl puppies.

CHAPTER 2
DECEMBER AFTERNOON

That afternoon the big box in the farmhouse kitchen was very quiet and lonely. Boomer still had his mother but without his sisters it was very silent. Since he was the only puppy left, the kind lady decided that he could come out to lay on the braided rug by the woodstove.

She stroked Boomer's head as he laid on the rug and pouted, his head between his legs. He sighed and gave the her his most pathetic look. He couldn't help but wonder if anyone would want him.

"You will just stay and live here with us, Boomer," the kind lady said. "You can be a herding dog like your father."

Boomer wouldn't mind staying with his mother and father, but he couldn't help but wonder if he was missing out on something. He wondered what adventures his sisters would go on while he stayed at the farm and worked the cattle.

The smell of pine filled the kitchen as the old gentleman of the house brought a pine tree through the door.

"Here's your Christmas tree, Dear," he said. "Only three days until Christmas I reckon we better get it up."

Boomer was suddenly interested. He roused himself from the rug in front the stove and trotted over to the tree. He sniffed the pine needles. This smelled different, therefore he decided he needed to pee on it to make it his. The elderly couple were talking and didn't notice Boomer until he had made a good size puddle on the wooden floor beside the tree. The lady stepped in the puddle in her stocking feet and turned to Boomer and gave him a scolding.

"I don't know, Pa, but I don't think this one is going to be gone by Christmas. We may just have to keep him."

The elderly gentleman looked troubled. "We already have a dog and two cats in the house. He will have to live with his father in the barn. He can stay in the house until Christmas but that's it."

Boomer did not quite understand the entire conversation but he was not at all pleased when he was put back in the box alone. He sulked in the corner of the box until he drifted off to a restless sleep.

CHAPTER 3
WHERE IS THE CORGI?

Boomer was having a strange dream. The kind that he knew he was dreaming but he just enjoyed the dream anyway and kept sleeping. He was flying through the night sky in a sleigh, riding in the seat beside a chubby old man with a long white beard.

The old man wore a red suit trimmed in white fur. He was quite jolly and laughed as he petted Boomer. He could smell the cold crisp night air. This dream was amazing.

Boomer opened one eye and started to yawn but something didn't seem right. He could not smell the pine Christmas tree any longer and he couldn't smell his mother. A whimper started to rise in his throat as he looked around the strange room.

Suddenly, a small face with pointed ears appeared before him. The little stranger wore a fluffy red jacket and a pointed hat and had his slender finger pressed to his lips to warn Boomer to be silent.

"You must not make a sound or you will ruin the surprise," the little elf whispered.

Boomer now had both eyes open wide. This was not the same house that he had come to know as home. There were no muddy boots by the door and he couldn't smell his mother or the earthy smell of the cattle that clung to the jackets of the elderly couple.

This house was quiet and new. There was a tall Christmas tree behind him. He could smell pine from the tree and cinnamon sticks from the kitchen and something else, something familiar. Yes, he knew that smell. It was the smell of a cat. He turned his head to see a fat tabby cat slowly approaching. The cat did not look at all pleased to see him. Boomer started to tremble as the cat arched her back and growled. Thankfully, the tiny elf came to his rescue.

"Don't mind Luna. She's a prima donna. She thinks she is the best thing that happened to this family. Just ignore her," the elf continued, "my name is Henry and I work for

Santa. I live here for the Holidays. You are here because two little girls asked Santa for a Corgi puppy for Christmas."

Boomer swallowed the whimper that had started to rise again in his throat. Everything was starting to make sense, and he wasn't so scared anymore. He now was glad that he wasn't adopted by one the families that had taken his sisters. It was so much more interesting to be a Christmas gift. He wondered what the two girls would be like. Would they like him or would he be too small? He closed his eyes while he pondered.

CHAPTER 4
CORGI'S NEW FAMILY

Boomer's eyes jerked wide open when he heard the slam of a car door and noisy footsteps in the kitchen. He raised his head from his little black and red dog bed, tempted to chew on the red bow tied neatly around his neck. He glanced up at Henry who was back on the mantle, sitting in a little sleigh, looking as much like a doll as he could. Henry gave him a stern look and Boomer dropped the bow from his mouth.

Two little girls came rushing over to the Christmas tree. They squealed with delight when they saw the Corgi puppy in front of the tree.

"Why is there a puppy in a bed in front of the tree?" the taller girl of the two asked, a puzzled look on her face, her straight blonde hair tucked neatly behind her ears. "Christmas is not until tomorrow."

The younger, smaller girl didn't say a word but bent down and gently stroked his head. She had very big brown eyes and short hair just a few shades darker than her sister's.

The parents looked at each other and smiled. "Santa told us that he had to deliver this little guy early," the father replied. "We told Santa that you wouldn't mind."

Both girls scrambled to hold the Corgi puppy. They started petting and kissing him. Though he wasn't used to the attention he thought that it was actually quite nice. He wagged his nub of a tail, catching on to their excitement.

"Look, his name is Boomer! It says so on the tag under the bow," the older girl observed.

Boomer took turns sitting in each girl's lap. He was the center of attention. They took him into the kitchen where they had set up a food dish and a water dish for him. The fat cat, Luna, looked at him from the counter top with disdain.

CHAPTER 5
WHAT IS THIS WHITE STUFF?

Traveling in Santa's sleigh had sure made him thirsty and did he ever have to pee! Boomer understood the word "puppy" and the word "outside", and noticed a shuffle of coats and the girls pulling on snow boots. Before he knew it he was scooped up in the arms of the older girl and transported out of the house to a small yard.

Outside was not what Boomer expected. There was curious cold white stuff on the ground and it stung his puppy paws. He picked up a paw and looked up at the older girl with his most pathetic face.

"Mommy, the puppy doesn't like the snow. He's shivering," the older girl opened up the door and yelled inside.

Soon the younger girl came running out of the house with a tiny blue and orange striped sweater in her hands.

"Look what mommy found under the Christmas tree," she exclaimed, "Santa must have known that Boomer would be cold."

The girls clumsily tried to pull the sweater over his head. Boomer bit playfully at the curious piece of clothing. Thank goodness the mom came outside and helped finish putting the sweater on him! He was much warmer now and didn't mind walking around the small front yard and sticking his nose in the snow. He did finally do his business and was praised loudly by the entire family.

Before he knew it he was back in the warm kitchen and the younger girl knelt down and placed a small bone in front of him. He settled down on the kitchen floor and started chewing.

He listed to his new family as they chatted at the dinner table. Boomer was satisfied as he chewed away. He closed his eyes as he listened to the sounds of his family talking and laughing.

CHAPTER 6
BEAUTY AND LUNA

The Christmas tree lights glowed and the Nutcracker played in the background as the family baked Christmas cookies. The girls soon got bored with decorating dozens of sugar cookie cutouts so a game of "chase the puppy" started. Boomer loved chasing the girls. They ran in circles through the house. On one of his laps chasing the girls Boomer ran into another cat. He was much happier to meet this cat than the cat was to meet him. The second cat was a calico named Beauty. She thought she was pretty special. He also learned that Beauty was Luna's younger sister.

Like her older sister, Beauty did not care for dogs. When Boomer accidently found himself nose to nose with her she arched her back and hissed, puffing up her long black and tan calico fur. She was quite terrifying. She was twice as big as him and with her long fluffy fur, she looked huge!

Boomer whined in fear. Fortunately, the older girl was right behind him and scooped him up safely in her arms.

"Knock it off, Beauty!" the older girl scolded.

Beauty gave the big girl an annoyed

look and strutted into the kitchen. Then both girls showered Boomer with attention all evening until it was time for them to go upstairs to bed. They placed a gate at the bottom of the stairs so Boomer had to stay in the living room. He was not happy about this but he was too tired to care. He was asleep as soon as his head hit the floor.

CHAPTER 7
CHRISTMAS EVE

Boomer was startled awake when he heard a sound coming from the chimney. Henry the elf jumped from the sleigh on the mantle where he had been sitting like a doll all evening when the family was awake.

"Santa's here!" Henry exclaimed in a

loud whisper.

A puff of soot and two black boots later, a round figure appeared in the living room. Santa looked at Boomer.

"Looks like you are doing well, little guy. How do you like this cold weather in Ohio?"

Boomer gave a small bark and a wiggle. Santa bent down and gave him a pat. So Ohio is where I am living now, Boomer thought to himself.

Boomer sat down and watched as Santa took green foil packages and red and white striped boxes and brightly colored bows from his big red velvet bag. There were so many packages and so many bows. The bows were what really interested Boomer. There were big bows, small bows, and long curly bows. Boomer really loved to chew and he thought he would really enjoy chewing on those bows.

Santa turned and walked over to the mantle and started filling the stockings with oranges, chocolates and small toys. Boomer walked over to one of the packages under the Christmas tree.

Maybe he could chew just one bow. No one would notice if one little bow was chewed and Santa was busy filling stockings, but before Boomer could get the bow fully in his mouth, Henry flew in front of him.

"Boomer you cannot chew the bows! I leave tonight with Santa and we have to trust you to be a good puppy."

Boomer looked up sheepishly at Henry but he gave the small elf a lick of agreement and reluctantly backed away from the packages.

Santa walked over to Boomer and picked him up.

"Merry Christmas, little guy. See you next year," he said as he gave him a pat and placed the small Corgi in his little dog bed.

Henry gave Boomer a wave goodbye and then jumped in Santa's velvet bag and just like that they both disappeared up the chimney. Boomer heard a jingle of sleigh bells in the distance and then all was silent in the house.

Luna, the fat cat, walked over to the Christmas tree and made herself comfortable in the middle of all the presents. He thought about barking at her but remembered that Henry had told him to be a good puppy so he closed his eyes and drifted off to sleep. He began dreaming about his new family.

CHAPTER 8
CHRISTMAS DAY

Boomer awoke to the sound of noisy feet running down the stairs. Both girls rushed to the Christmas tree and started talking excitedly at the same time. Luna lay on the back of the couch and Beauty looked down from her perch on the cat tree. Boomer was feeling very full of pee and thought he may have an accident at any moment. Thankfully, the mom calmed the girls down enough for them to pull on boots and coats and take him outside first. After the quick trip to the snow covered front yard Boomer was back in the house and ready to participate in the Christmas craziness.

First, each family member took down their stocking from the mantle. They took out oranges and chocolate bars, socks and small toys. These things were put on the couch so Boomer could not reach them. He stretched his chubby white legs up on the side of the couch and tried to smell the oranges and chocolate.

"No, No, Boomer," the youngest girl softly told him. "Chocolate is bad for dogs. It would make you very sick."

She lifted the small corgi in her arms and carried him over to the Christmas tree.

"You can help me open my presents," she said.

Boomer liked this idea and took his teeth and helped tear off the wrapping paper on a big box wrapped in red foil paper. Soon Boomer was running from girl to girl "helping" pull off wrapping paper and bows. He even got a couple good chews in on some bows before they were snatched from his mouth.

After all the presents were unwrapped Boomer jumped in the big pile of paper and rolled on his back. Then both girls brought him a red plaid stocking that had the letter B on it.

"Boomer, Santa left this stocking for you. Let's see what goodies are inside!" the older girl exclaimed. Boomer sniffed the stocking and the girls pulled out two dog biscuits that looked like Christmas cookies. Then he saw a plush striped candy cane. He pulled it out with his teeth. It squeaked when he bit down on it which he found very amusing. The little girl tickled his feet and they played tug of war with the candy cane.

CHAPTER 9
BOOMER BELONGS

After the wrapping paper was cleared away and Boomer had his breakfast he settled down for a nap. Bing Crosby Christmas songs played on the stereo as the girls played with their new toys. Boomer was much too tired to join in the fun, for he was a very small puppy and needed his nap. He laid down beside the couch and was fast asleep in no time.

Boomer didn't know how long he had been sleeping but the smell of something wonderful made him wake up. He smelled roast beef! Oh, how he loved roast beef. Back at the farm where he was born the old lady and gentleman had fed him scraps of roast beef for a treat.

He waddled over to where the mom and dad were cooking in the kitchen, but they were too busy to notice him. Boomer gave a sharp little bark. The mom jumped and then looked down at him.

"Looks like the puppy wants some roast beef, Honey," she remarked to the dad.

The dad bent down with a small piece of beef, "Here you go little guy." Boomer happily retreated under the kitchen table to enjoy the delicious meat.

CHAPTER 10
WHAT HAPPENS NOW?

After Christmas dinner Boomer and the girls went outside to play in the white stuff. Boomer learned that it was called "snow". The girls rode in a large plastic tray down piles of snow with the Corgi puppy riding in their laps. It was great fun. He learned that the tray was called a "sled".

These humans had funny names for things, Boomer thought to himself. The girls then scooped up the snow with their hands to form little balls. They threw these balls at each other and Boomer.

This game was very entertaining to Boomer. He never once got hit with a snowball. He could dodge, run and sidestep and no one could hit him, not even the mom and dad of his family. Then, all too soon, it was time to go back inside the house. The older girl reached down to pick up Boomer. He, however, was not ready to go inside. He had other plans. The youngest girl started chasing him in an effort to help.

Boomer saw this as an opportunity to show of his dodging skills. In no time the girls were chasing the naughty puppy through the snow. Luckily for the girls, Corgis have short legs and the effort of trying to run through the deep snow tired him quickly. The younger girl succeeded in snagging him and he was plopped in the entryway of the house.

After a snack and some water, Boomer found his doggy bed and settled down for his afternoon nap. He was very tired. Today had been the most exciting day of his little puppy life. He sighed his little content Corgi sigh and laid his head on his paws. "I wonder what tomorrow will be like," he thought to himself as his eyes began to close.

Little did he know what his family had in store for him in the weeks to come.

To be continued…

ABOUT THE AUTHOR

N. W. Nelson grew up on a farm in rural Ohio.
She graduated Magna Cum Laude from Ohio
University with a Master of Arts in Spanish. She
earned her B.A. in Spanish as well from Ohio
University. She has lived in Merida, Mexico and
taught for Ohio University's Programa Mayab.
She currently lives in central Ohio with her spouse
and two daughters. Their entire family loves all
types of animals, domestic and wild. They have a
wide variety of pets in addition to their two
adorable Welsh Pembroke Corgis.

Made in the USA
Lexington, KY
11 December 2019